THE MAN IN THE IRON MASK

Vol. 2: High Treason

Adapted from the novel by ALEXANDRE DUMAS

THE STORY SO FAR:

n the 17th century, **Athos, Porthos,** and **Aramis**—famed as "The Three Musketeers"—
e joined in friendship by young **d'Artagnan,** who eventually joined their fabled ranks in
vice to the King of France.

ome three decades later, Athos had become a count—currently held in disfavor by young
ng Louis XIV—while Porthos had been named a landed baron, and shrewd Aramis a
n of the cloth. Only d'Artagnan remained in the rank of the Musketeers, which he now
nmanded.

ramis—now Bishop of Vannes—learned that one **Philippe "Marchiali,"** a prisoner in the
stille, was actually King Louis' twin brother. Since birth, he had been hidden away, lest
owledge of his existence cause a civil war. To free him, Aramis enlisted the unwitting aid of
incredibly wealthy **Nicolas Fouquet,** the King's Surintendant (collector of taxes), to free
ilippe and keep him in hiding for a few days.

leanwhile, Fouquet feared that his rival, the finance minister **Jean-Baptiste Colbert,**
emes to undermine his position with the King. Aramis convinced him to schedule a
gantuan fête (festival) at his vast estate, Vaux-le-Vicomte, in the King's honor...hoping
gain the royal favor. But Aramis had an agenda all his own....

Writer
Roy Thomas

Special Thanks
Deborah Sherer & Freeman Henry

Penciler
Hugo Petrus

Inker
Tom Palmer

Colorist
June Chung

Letterer
Virtual Calligraphy's Joe Caramagna

Cover
Marko Djurdjevic

Special Thanks
Chris Allo

Production
acob Chabot

Associate Editor
Nicole Boose

Editor
Ralph Macchio

Editor in Chief
Joe Quesada

Publisher
Dan Buckley

VISIT US AT
www.abdopublishing.com

Reinforced library bound edition published in 2009 by Spotlight, a division of the ABDO Group, 8000 West 78th Street, Edina, Minnesota 55439. Spotlight produces high-quality reinforced library bound editions for schools and libraries. Published by agreement with Marvel Characters, Inc.

Library of Congress Cataloging-in-Publication Data

Thomas, Roy, 1940-
The man in the iron mask / adapted from the novel by Alexandre Dumas ; Roy Thomas, writer ; Hugo Petrus, penciler ; Tom Palmer, inker ; Virtual Calligraphy's Joe Caramagna, letterer ; June Chung, colorist. -- Reinforced library bound ed.
v. cm.
"Marvel."
Contents: v. 1. The three musketeers -- v. 2. High treason -- v. 3. The iron mask -- v. 4. The man in the iron mask -- v. 5. The death of a titan -- v. 6. Musketeers no more.
ISBN 9781599615943 (v. 1) -- ISBN 9781599615950 (v. 2) -- ISBN 978159961596 (v. 3) -- ISBN 9781599615974 (v. 4) -- ISBN 9781599615981 (v. 5) -- ISBN 9781599615998 (v. 6)
Summary: Retells, in comic book format, Alexandre Dumas' tale of political intrigue romance, and adventure in seventeenth-century France.
[1. Dumas, Alexandre, 1802-1870.--Adaptations. 2. Graphic novels. 3. Adventure and adventurers--Fiction. 4. France--History--Louis XIII, 1610-1643--Fiction.] I. Dumas, Alexandre, 1802-1870. II. Petrus, Hugo. VI. Title.
PZ7.7.T518 Man 2009
[Fic]--dc22 2008035321

All Spotlight books have reinforced library bindings and are manufactured in the United States of America.

15 August...the day preceding the fête given by Monsieur Fouquet:
The youthful King was most eager for amusements... and thus very desirous to arrive at Vaux-le-Vicomte as early as possible.
For only twice during the journey had he been able to catch a glimpse of his beloved, Louise de la Vallière...
...and he suspected that his only opportunity of speaking to her might be after nightfall, in the gardens of the château.
Thus, he had left most of his enormous entourage behind at Mélun, and would arrive at Vaux relatively unescorted.
"We go to see a friend as friends," the King had declared.

D'Artagnan, captain of the Musketeers, had encouraged his sovereign in this action...
...saying that M. Fouquet, the master of Vaux, was a man of honor.

All the same, certain questions welled up within d'Artagnan.
Why had his old friend Aramis, now Bishop of Vannes, been so interested recently in seeing the King's new costumes for the fête?
And why, of late, had he become so mixed up in the affairs of Surintendant Fouquet, collector of taxes?
He had no doubt that Aramis had some motive in that...
...and he resolved to address himself directly to his erstwhile Musketeer comrade, when next they met.
What could Aramis' object possibly be-- unless it were to overthrow Fouquet's rival, M. Colbert?
Within the carriage bearing the Queen and the Queen-Mother, King Louis frowned, recalling an earlier conversation with his finance minister, M. Colbert...
Surely Your Majesty will sleep here in Mélun, and proceed to Vaux in the morning.
What? When M. Fouquet is expecting us this evening?
You other gentlemen may go slowly... but we will ride on.
Louis had known that Colbert merely wished to cause annoyanc to M. Fouquet, who was anxiously awaiting the royal party's arrival.

Meanwhile, at Vaux-le-Vicomte, though we've no record of it, Aramis must surely have conversed thus with Porthos, now a baron...
Wonderful to see you again, old friend.
Ah, Porthos-- how long it's been since those days when you, Athos, and I were hailed as "The Three Musketeers"-- and d'Artagnan as the fourth!
I fear I am both lder...and stouter.
I encouraged my valet to eat well, till he equaled my girth--so my tailors could measure him, instead of myself.
But you are still what they called you then..."The Hercules of France."
And the country has dire need once more of us both.
Is something amiss, Aramis?
Is that why you asked me to come to Vaux twenty-four hours before His Majesty's arrival?
Yes, mon ami.
I have uncovered... a plot against the King!
What?
A most heinous plot-- which only you and I may hope to foil.
I have discovered that the King has been replaced on the throne by an imposter-- a double!
Is such a thing possible?

Not just possible. Accomplished!
And you and I must place the crown again upon the proper brow.
What must I do to help?
When the time comes, you must obey my commands without question.
Yes, my friend... certainly.
Without question!
Together, we will save the King--and France!

Ah, to be again the champion of France--as in the old days!
Men may yet erect a statue of me--
--and, of course, of you, as well, dear Aramis!

At seven o'clock in the evening, without announcing his arrival by the din of trumpets, and without most of his advance guard...
...the King presented himself before the magnificent gates of Vaux...
...where M. and Mme. Fouquet had been waiting for the last half-hour.

You have had the roads put in excellent order, M. Fouquet.
A stone is hardly to be found the size of an egg the whole way from Mélun to Vaux, Your Majesty.

I wished it to be as if your carriage were rolling along upon a carpet.
And so, indeed, it was, sir.

At once, any lingering suspicions that d'Artagnan may have had concerning Fouquet's motives disappeared.
"M. Fouquet," he said to himself, "is the man for me."

We do not intend to describe the grand banquet, at which all the royal guests were present, including M. Colbert...though not the Bishop of Vannes or the Baron Porthos.
It will suffice to note that the King's countenance soon went, from being gay, to wearing a gloomy and irritated expression.
He remembered that his own residence, royal though it was, was merely an historical monument of earlier days, the relic of his predecessors.
Fouquet ate from a gold service, and drank wines of which the King of France did not even know the name...
...out of goblets each more precious than the whole royal cellar.
Louis' eyes filled with tears.
He dared not look at his Queen.

When the supper was finished, the King expressed a desire to walk in the illuminated park...
...accompanied only by d'Artagnan and M. Fouquet.

And now the fête was complete in every respect...

...for the King was able to have a "chance encounter" with La Vallière...

...to walk a little while with her in one of the winding paths of the wood...

...and press her hand...
I love you.

...without anyone overhearing him...

...except, of course, for d'Artagnan and M. Fouquet.

The night of magical enchantments stole on.
While the Queens passed to their own apartments, accompanied by the music of theorbos and lutes...
Let me show you, Your Majesty, to your own bedroom...

...the chamber of Morpheus.

M. d'Herbay* oversaw totally the redesign of this part of the château.

I hope you will enjoy the vaulted ceiling, painted by the famous Lebrun...

*Aramis' formal name.

...and depicting the happy, as well as disagreeable, dreams with which that legendary god of sleep affects kings as well as other men.
You shiver, Your Majesty. Is the room too cold?
I...am sleepy, that is all.

till...would you have he goodness to tell M. Colbert I wish to see him?
Of course, sire.

D'Artagnan, for his part, determined to lose no time in finding his former comrade, the Bishop of Vannes...

...in that worthy's own chamber, called the Blue Room...
Well, Aramis...

...and so we have come to Vaux.
Ah d'Artagnan! I have been engaged about the theatrical performances to take place tomorrow.

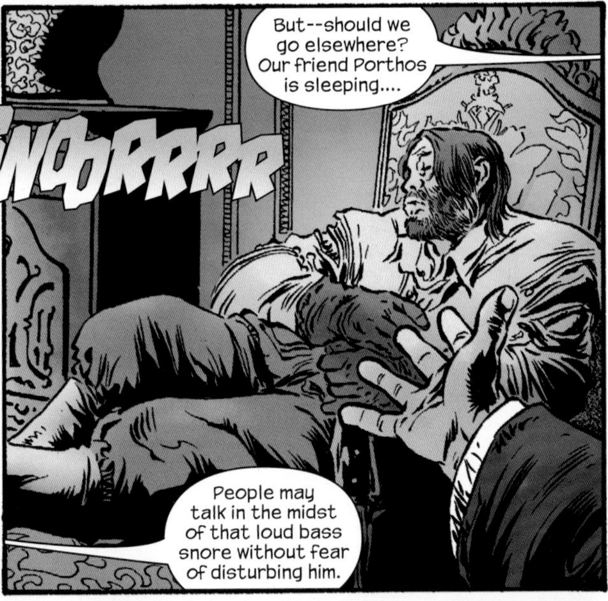
But--should we go elsewhere? Our friend Porthos is sleeping....
SNOORRRR
People may talk in the midst of that loud bass snore without fear of disturbing him.

You are the omptroller-eneral of the Fêtes here, then?
You know I am a friend of all kinds of amusement wherein the exercise of imagination is required.

For which reason, I must be close to the King.
The flooring of my room is merely the covering of his ceiling.

Aramis...I must voice what I feel. I fear you conspire against the King.
What? If I have not the firm intention of making tomorrow the most glorious day my King has ever enjoyed--may Heaven's lightning blast me where I stand!

Then why did you take some patterns of His Majesty's costumes from his tailor?
So I could have a accurate portrait the King painted and present it here.

You will see it on the morrow.
The earnestness of your words soothes my heart. I take my leave.

Please wake Porthos and take him with you...for he snores like a park of artillery.
I shall.
SNORRR

Good night, my friends. In ten minutes I shall b fast asleep.

As soon as his two former comrades had left, Aramis bolted the door...
Monseigneur! Monseigneur!
M. d'Artagnan entertains a great many suspicions, it seems.
Philippe pushed aside a sliding panel behind the bed...

He is very devoted to...*me.*

If d'Artagnan does not recognize you before the other has disappeared...
...you ma rely upon h to the en of the wor

Now, my lord, ke up your post t our place of bservation...

...and watch the King's actions...

...through these openings.

They answer to one of the false windows...

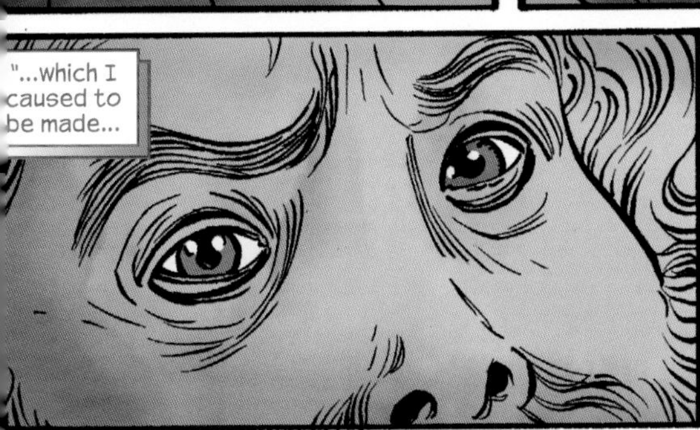
"...which I caused to be made...

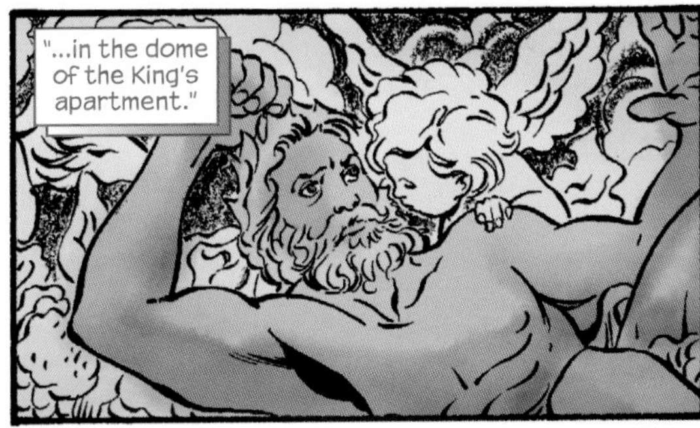
"...in the dome of the King's apartment."

"Bishop! He has a visitor--I recognize the finance minister!"
This letter, written by the late Cardinal Mazarin, will prove to Your Majesty that thirteen million livres have been given to M. Fouquet.
A tolerably good sum, Colbert.
These thirteen millions have never been returned...
...for M. Fouquet used them to erect this great estate.

They are, no doubt, paying for this very fête.
Mazarin's letter proves it so, Majesty.
If this is true...

It is late. By morning, I shall have made up my mind what to do about M. Fouquet.
But...
Very good, sire.

"The King has given himself time for reflection..."

Now watch, monseigneur, and study well...
...how a King retires to his rest.

History has told us of the various events of the following day and night... of the splendid fêtes given by the Surintendant to his sovereign.
There was a promenade... a banquet...a comedy to be acted.
Full of preoccupation, however, the King showed himself cold, reserved, and taciturn

Nothing could smooth the frown upon his face...
M. Fouquet observed that deep resentment, rising from the depths of the King's heart...
...and was sorely troubled.

Later that evening, the King and M. Colbert walked in the park...
...where La Vallière contrive to meet her lovin sovereign.

What sadness so clearly oppresses Your Majesty?
M. Colbert has informed me that M. Fouquet has stolen moneys which belong to me...
...and I have decided to have our host arrested.

In his own house, sire? Will not such an act dishonor you, far more than him?
Mademoiselle, it almost seems you defend this traitor!

It is not M. Fouquet I am defending, sire, but yourself. You--
Majesty-- Mademoiselle-- someone comes!
Leave me, Louise.

As you wish, sire.

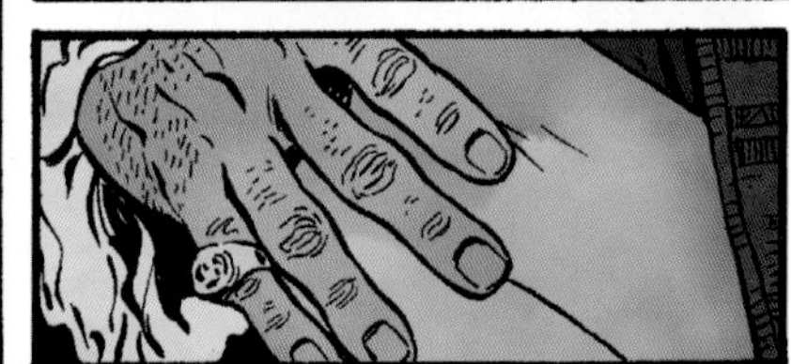

Ah! Mademoiselle de la Vallière has let something fall.
What is it?

A paper...
A letter...
Something white. Look there, sire.

The King picked up the letter, meaning to read it later...just as the torch-bearers arrived, making the darkness as bright as day.

Hardly had the King returned to the château, than a mass of fire burst from the dome of Vaux, illuminating the remotest corners.
The fireworks had begun.
Ere long, the King remembered the letter...
...which, he believed, La Vallière had dropped as she hurried away.
A death-like pallor stole over his face... as he read a love letter, sent by M. Fouquet to La Vallière, long before...
...and which had recently fallen into-- and from--the hands of M. Colbert.

Minutes afterward, d'Artagnan entered Louis XIV's apartment.
How many men will be required to arrest M. Fouquet?
Arrest M. Fouquet? It is so easy that a mere child might do it.
Still, Your Majesty will forgive me, but, in order to effect this arrest...

...I should like written instructions...

...in case, when your anger passes, you regret your actions.

Since when has the King's word been insufficient for you?
Arrest him, and hold him until the morning...

...when I shall have made up my mind what I shall do with him!
I...will do as you command, sire.

After d'Artagnan had quitted the room...
Fouquet squanders my finances...
...and now tries to rob me of the one to whom I am most attached!

I hate him--I hate him--I hate him!
Tomorrow, people shall see what utter ruin a King's anger shall have wrought!

Almost weeping, he threw himself upon his bed...

...and soon, absolute silence reigned in the chamber of Morpheus.

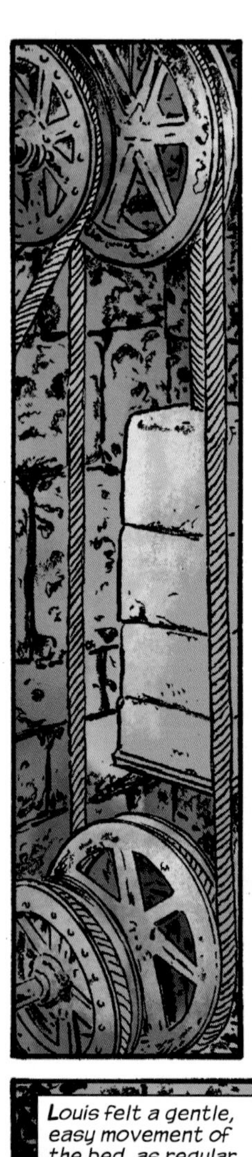

Then it seemed to the King...

...as if the dome...

...gradually receded...
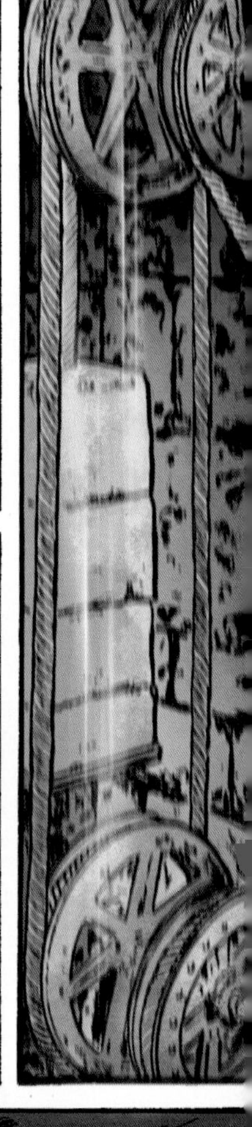

...and that the painted figures...

...became darker and darker...

...as the distance became more and more remote.

Louis felt a gentle, easy movement of the bed, as regular as that by which a vessel plunges beneath the waves...
I am under the influence of a terrible dream...

...as the last light of the royal chamber faded away, as if he were descending toward the bottom of a well...

And then the bed stopped.
It is time to awaken from this dream.
Come! Let me wake up!

And then he perceived that he was already awake...

...and that two men, each masked, stood silently at his bedside.
What is this, monsieur?
What is the meaning of this jest?

It is no jest.

Do you belong to M. Fouquet?

It matters very little to whom we belong.
We are your masters now--that is sufficient.

Is this--a dungeon?
No...a subterranean passage.
Will you be good enough to follow us?
I shall not stir from hence!
If you are obstinate, my dear young friend...
I will lift you up in my arms and roll you up in a cloak.
And if you are stifled there, why, so much the worse for you!
It seems... I have fallen into the hands of a pair of assassins.

Tell me, at least, where we are going.

Come.

Unnhh! You dare to shove me thus?
What do you intend to do with the King of France?

Try to forget that word.
You deserve to be broken on the wheel for using that word... but the King is too kind-hearted.

Get in.

In the early hours of the morning, after having called out to the sentinel, "By the King's order!"...
...the driver conducted the horses into the circular enclosure of the Bastille.

THWAM THWAM THWAM

What is the matter now?
Who have you...

...brought me?

Monsieur d'Herblay!
Hush. Let us go inside.

And fire at once if he speaks!
Very good!

Dear Bishop--Aramis--what brings you here at this hour?
It appears, my dear M. de Baisemeaux, that you were quite right the other evening.
We both thought it called for the release of Marchiali...

But, as you see, it is that poor Scotch fellow Seldon whom the King wishes set at liberty.
Indeed, so it says!
But you convinced me the order referred to Marchiali.

I am a lost man--releasing the wrong prisoner!
No. Since I have brought Marchiali back, it is as if he had never left.
You will lock him up at once--and you will release Seldon. Do you understand?
I--I--
Very good.
The man in the carriage--who did not speak for fear of being shot--was quickly brought into the Bastille...
...and locked in the very cell in which Philippe had, for six long years, bemoaned his existence.
You noticed the resemblance between that unfortunate wretch and--
And the King? Yes!
Well, the very first use he made of his freedom was to dress himself like the King--and pretend he was the King!
Gracious Heavens! I shall go set Seldon free...
Tomorrow will be time enough.
Remember--no one is to enter Marchiali's cell, except with an order from the King--
--an order I will myself bring.

Now, Porthos, my good fellow...
Back again to Vaux, and as fast as possible!

A man is light and easy enough, when he has faithfully served his King...

...and, in serving him, saved his country!

Thus did the young King come to pass the night in the chill of the dungeon...

...even as Philippe lay in restful sleep at Vaux-le-Vicomte...

...beneath the royal canopy.